15165

A\

E
Kra

Kraus, Robert
How Spider saved the
baseball game

DATE DUE			
JAN 13 1990			
JAN 2 9 1990			
FEB 1			
JUL 2 6 1991			
JAN 27 1992			
JUL 2 2 1992			
AUG 2 4 1992			
SEP 16 1992			
AUG - 5 1993			

HOW Spider SAVED THE Baseball Game

BUG LEAGUE

BY
ROBERT KRAUS

SCHOLASTIC INC.

New York Toronto London Auckland Sydney

ISBN 0-590-41791-6

12 11 10 9 8 7 6 5 4 3 2 1   9/8 0 1 2 3 4/9

Printed in the U.S.A.   23

First Scholastic printing, April 1989

15165

It was the first day of the baseball season, and I was feeling sad. Fly didn't choose me to play on his baseball team.

I came to the game anyway. If I couldn't play, I could cheer.

"Thank goodness you're here, Spider," said Fly. "Ladybug and I are the only bugs who showed up."

"What position can you play?" asked Fly.
"We have lots of openings."

"Try me," I said.

I couldn't catch fly balls.

I couldn't catch ground balls.

I was a slow runner

and I couldn't hit.

"You can't hit, field, or catch," said Fly. "You be the pitcher. I'll catch and Ladybug will play first base."

"Since we have no infield or outfield, you'll have to pitch a no-hitter."

"Hand me the ball," I said.
I took a few warm-up tosses to see if
I had my stuff. I had my stuff!
The old spider ball was working.

The Bedbug All Stars took the field.

What a great team they had!
Babe Bedbug, Reggie Bedbug, Mookie
Bedbug. All Slugger bugs!

Mayor Bugg threw out
the first ball.

"Play ball!" yelled Miss Quito the umpire.

Babe Bedbug, the home run king, was up first.
"Boo," booed Fly.
"Be a good sport," said Ladybug.
"I will be as long as we win," said Fly.

Babe was no match for my spider ball.
He fanned on three straight pitches.
I set the side down, one, two, three.

The Bedbug pitcher was Bobby Bedbug.
He was throwing fastballs at one hundred
miles an hour.

Fly, Ladybug, and I all struck out.
It was a pitcher's duel.

Scoreless inning followed scoreless inning.

The game was getting so boring,
fans were leaving or falling asleep.

It was inning eight. The score was
Bedbugs 0, Fly's Guys 0.
Babe Bedbug popped up, but
thank goodness, Ladybug caught it!

It was the top of the ninth. I was tiring.
Throwing spider balls is not easy.
I knew I could not go on much longer.

I came to bat in the bottom of the ninth.
The score was still 0-0. One run would win it.
What a spot to be in. And me a .00 hitter.

The fans went wild.
I had to come through.
Rapid Robert fired one in.

I swung for the fences and missed.
"STRIKE ONE!" yelled Miss Quito.

I dug in at the plate.
Rapid Robert fired another one.
I took a tremendous swing...and missed.
"Strike Two!" yelled Miss Quito.

"Do your thing, Spider!" yelled Fly, coaching from the sidelines.
Rapid Robert fired the ball in.
I did my thing.
I got hit by the pitch.
"Take your base!" yelled Miss Quito.

I was standing on first base, but it was still a long way
to home plate.

Fly was batting.
He was supposed to hit,
and I was supposed to run.
He missed but I ran anyway.

Yogi Bedbug, the catcher, threw the ball to second base.
It went over the second basebug's head.

I rounded second base and ran at top speed to third base. The center fielder juggled the ball, and I headed for home!

"Slide, Spider, slide!" screamed Ladybug.
"SAFE!" yelled Miss Quito.
"We won!" screamed Fly.

"You saved the baseball game, Spider," said Ladybug.
"You did," said Fly. "I cannot tell a lie."
"You're not a Bedbug," said Babe, "but you're an
All Star."
I was very happy to be me.

THE END